Hazel the Hedgehog

Rachel McKay

Written, illustrated and published by Rachel McKay.

www.mckaybookstore.com

Hazel once went out to play

on a cold and rainy day

Then she went out to look
for some food,

something to make her
tunny feel good.

As hard as she tried, she found not a thing.

Not a bug, or a slug,
not anything.

"I'm so cold!" she said,
"what will I do?"

"I'm wet, and I'm tired
and I'm hungry too!"

"It must be time to sleep" she said.

"And wake again in spring instead."

"Hang on Hazel, you'll need to wait!"

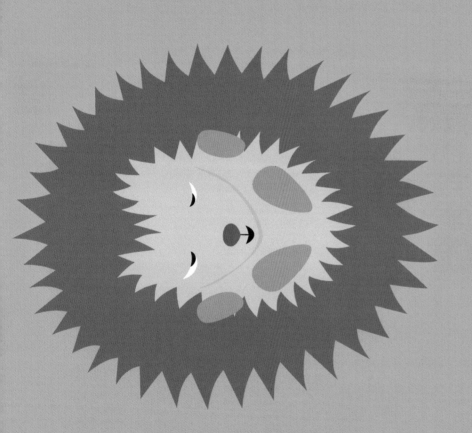

"You're much too small to hibernate!"

"What" cried Hazel,
"I'm too small?"

"The food
I had,
I ate
it all!"

"I don't know what to do she cried, I've looked so hard, I've tried and tried!"

Hazel looked, and looked, and looked, and looked, all night.

There was no food, just none in sight!

Hazel crossed the road

and followed the path.

into the garden and

right past the bird bath.

No food, no bugs or slugs
at all.

Poor Hazel curled up
in a ball.

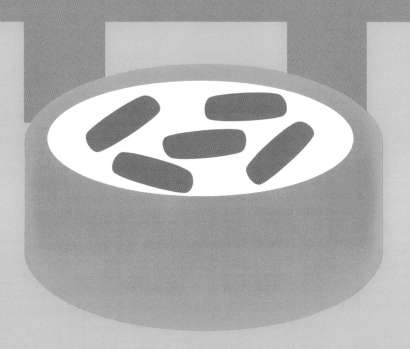

Then she saw it,
with her own eyes.

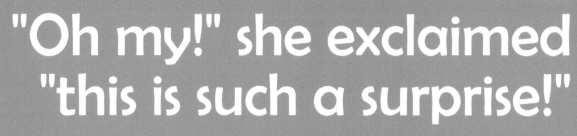

"Oh my!" she exclaimed
"this is such a surprise!"

At the end of the path, there was a small dish.

Just what she wanted, she now had her wish!

The food was so yummy,
had such a nice taste!

Hazel ate all she could,
and left nothing to waste.

Looking for more, she came back the next night.

Seeing more food, she was filled with delight!

She came back to that
dish every day for a week.

Her future now looking,
not quite so bleak.

She ate more and more,
and got bigger, and stronger.

No need for Hazel to
wait any longer!

Sleep tight Hazel, we'll see you in spring when the little bees buzz and little birds sing.